# CHLORINE
# SKY

CROWN

NEW YORK

# CHLORINE SKY

# SKY

MAHOGANY L. BROWNE

Text copyright © 2021 by Mahogany L. Browne
Jacket art copyright © 2021 by Kgabo "Saint Rose" Mametja
All rights reserved. Published in the United States by
Crown Books for Young Readers, an imprint of Random House Children's Books,
a division of Penguin Random House LLC, New York.

Crown and the colophon are registered trademarks of Penguin Random House LLC.

Visit us on the Web! GetUnderlined.com

Educators and librarians, for a variety of teaching tools,
visit us at RHTeachersLibrarians.com

*Library of Congress Cataloging-in-Publication Data*
Names: Browne, Mahogany L., author.
Title: Chlorine sky / Mahogany L. Browne.
Description: First edition. | New York: Crown Books for Young Readers,
[2021] | Audience: Ages 14+. | Audience: Grades 10–12. | Summary: Picked on at home, criticized for talking trash while beating boys at basketball, and always seen as less than her best friend, a girl struggles to like and accept herself.
Identifiers: LCCN 2020035685 (print) | LCCN 2020035686 (ebook) |
ISBN 978-0-593-17639-9 (hardcover) | ISBN 978-0-593-17640-5 (library binding) |
ISBN 978-0-593-17641-2 (ebook)
Subjects: CYAC: Novels in verse. | Self-esteem—Fiction. | Friendship—Fiction. |
Sisters—Fiction. | Basketball—Fiction. | Dating (Social customs)—Fiction. |
African Americans—Fiction.
Classification: LCC PZ7.5.B774 Chl 2021 (print) | LCC PZ7.5.B774 (ebook) |
DDC [Fic]—dc23

The text of this book is set in 10.75-point Adobe Garamond.
Interior design by Jen Valero
Printed in the United States of America
10 9 8 7 6 5 4
First Edition

*to my grandmothers:*
*thank you for teaching me kindness*

*to my younger self:*
*you deserve, you deserve, you deserve*

*to my daughter:*
*you are the most beautiful poem i've ever written*

# CHLORINE
# SKY

## ME & LAY LI AIN'T TALKING

cause she think she cute

cause she think I ain't.

Must be pretty boy Curtis

all in her head

all in her mouth

making her forget

her home training.

Making her forget

her daddy got a gun for a living.

    & her mama gone.

## & THIS IS WHY I THINK

she ain't got no sense, nohow.

Cause ain't nobody but fast girls

checking for Curtis.

& he keep her name close

& she don't come home

the same way no more.

She must think she cute!

Must think I ain't!

Like she *ZendayaSkaiStormMeganNickiBeyoncé* or something

Like she long curly hair movie star perfect

Like she perfect pink nail salon pop queen perfect

Like she all new Macy's rack & Adidas shell toe perfect

Like she glossy magazine cover most beautiful girl perfect

Like she ain't never had a bad day in the sun perfect

Like she ain't never had a bad picture kind of perfect

Like she got a life don't nobody judge cause she's so perfect

I mean,

look how she keep me waiting like

I'm supposed to wait on Curtis

or something

& I hate his light-skinned self!

Especially because he ain't as funny

as he think.

Especially when he calls me black

& ugly & stupid!

## & LAY LI STAY GRINNING

like he the sun

like we ain't friends

they boyfriends see Lay Li

    It's like they see the best parts of they favorite movie

& they favorite movie got they favorite soundtrack

& they favorite soundtrack make them feel strong

& they swing they arms around & show off to whoever is looking

    I mean, sometimes I get caught looking
    but I ain't got n o t h i n g to say

Not Lay Li

She act like she never lookin'

She must think she cute

But she ain't just cute

Lay Li pretty

& they boyfriends at the skate rink

forget they home training around her.

So when Curtis say the things

I've already said about myself

& she laugh

I know deep down inside

she ain't never care about me at all.

## LAY LI THE SUN

& she called me best friend

Called me smart

Called me her ace

Called me her right-hand sis

Lay Li called me my name

Ain't never call me nothing but my name

When everyone else call me nothing

She say best friend—like sis-patna-friend & she laugh bright *bright*

Because Lay Li the sun

now I know she just said them lies

to keep my shadow

all up & around her sunshine smile

## LIKE THAT TIME WE SKIPPED SCHOOL

for the pool party

& all the girls wear bikinis

but I got my one-piece on

with a white T-shirt on top.

& the boys just looking

like they mama ain't taught them nothing worth knowing.

Lay Li got that good hair

so she don't care if it's wet & loose.

But my hair ain't close to being good

so I keep it in a real real real tight ponytail

until the sun get so hot

I jump in & cool my sadness down.

It's like I already know.

So I let my shoulders sink low

like my heart be

& I watch Lay Li

how she walks & everybody stops

& I'm trying to learn

how to walk in a room & turn their heads

how to move in a crowd & be the light

how to keep a boy's interest

    but not just any boy

    a boy who remembers my name

    maybe a cute one with long eyelashes

    & gentle hands

    the kind of hands that keep to themselves

how to keep my sister, Essa, from talking bad to me

my older sister tell you "don't mess up my name,"

she go so far to move her mouth & show her perfect white teeth

it's "EEEEEE-SaaHHHH like mantra, like a prayer"

how to move through the world

*standing* tall & demanding to be named properly

how to be more than a baller

how to be someone that keep 'em guessing

how to stop stressing because ain't nobody

got time for the kind of shade I got

but everybody got time for some

s   u   n

## LAY LI SMILE AT CURTIS

& he only a little bit cute

but he ain't funny or smart

so that's how I know her grin is a lie.

& I pretend I don't hear his slur

I pretend I don't see his hazel eyes

when he say "lose her ugly black ass"

& Lay Li laugh.

    Laugh like a knife in the back or laugh hysterical like the girl
    running from the scary man in a hockey mask or laugh like
    kids being followed around the mall by security or laugh like
    I do when my sister, Essa, makes me the butt of the joke.
    She laugh & laugh & laugh & laugh &

she say "Shut up, Curtis"

but it sounds like     "Come here."

I dunk my head underwater slow

& wait

    just wait

        I wait even longer

for her to say a n y t h i n g like:

"don't talk about my friend, I don't care how pretty
your eyes is!"

But she just say "shut up"

& she l a u g h

the kind of laugh that make me forget

we even friends

the kind of laugh that make me forget

we even

& I think

*I could stay here*

where it's all a blurry aqua blue,

I think

*I could* stay here

where my eyes

don't hurt as much

& it don't feel

like I've been looking at the sun

all day l o n g.

## OKAY, SO BOOM. THIS IS HOW LAY LI & I MET.

At the end of summer, when we ready to head into
the first semester of freshman year, I got a problem

with the boys who keep slapping the water.
Tyrone & Adam slap the water at me

when I swim by them. Because everybody knows
I'm better than them on the basketball court.

Still, I keep calm. I play cool. I see a girl at the edge
of the pool. Red swimsuit & long wavy ponytail.

Her right eyebrow lifted skylike: She ready
for the joke. But she ain't laughing.

The boys slap the water. I swim under
the current. I head to her side of the pool.

& so do they. They slap the water but
her mouth ain't like mine. It ain't closed

lock-like & tight, until I'm on the court
with a nasty dribble. It ain't safety pin safe

like my grandmother taught me. Her mouth
curse them until their eyes water. Her lips

curl & she cross both her arms
"& you betta not do it again!" They laugh

& she don't. This girl I never seen before
got a name: Lay Li.

I wipe my eyes, stinging from the blue water.
"Thank you," I say, pretending it don't burn.

## TWO YEARS LATER & LAY LI BATHING SUIT

Is way better than mine

I hate my royal blue one-piece

It's a hand-me-down

It's ugly

I rather wear my basketball shorts

but they're the only pair I got

keep dry when I walk home

Everybody who know somebody

will skip class for the pool party

& everybody will have a cute bathing suit on:

Strawberry red

or bright yellow

or periwinkle blue

or one of those two-pieces with candy cane stripes

But not me

## I PUT A T-SHIRT ON TOP

& try to hide

this ugly-ass basic blue swimsuit

Mines is long in the crotch

so long the water drains slowly down my leg

after I climb out the deep end.

I put a T-shirt on top

& try to hide the history

of where my people from

the ones that got a pit bull with a chain around its neck
& smoke clouds everywhere

I put a T-shirt on top

& try to hide where I come from

the kind of folks that park on the lawn & clean they car

with the Gap Band blasting out the door speakers

I put a T-shirt on top

& hope no one asks where my dad works.

Where my dad is?

Why my sister, Essa, & I always fight on the lawn?

I just want to swim

in the teal green sorta blue bubble

& forget all the things that make me different

for a little while.

## BASKETBALL DRILLS #1

both hands grip the orange world

ridges in black talk back to my fingertips

James

Bird

Bryant

Catchings

Jordan

Leslie

Curry

Hammon

Jackson

Iverson

Johnson

For every letter of their name

I plant my feet aim & shoot

if I flick my left wrist perfectly

I'll soar like the greats.

## AFTER MY DRILLS

Lay Li & I both sit in the shade

on the front lawn of the neighborhood candy house

Miss Irene got white hair & a permanent scowl

She got white hair, a little white lapdog & wear a dusty muumuu

She smokes cigarettes, the white stick hanging
from the cliff of her lip

Like a daredevil

Miss Irene say she ain't got time for us kids

& don't let nobody curse on her front yard

But she got a Costco card & charge pennies on the dollar

for our favorite sweets

We get a dollar worth of candy in a plastic sandwich bag

that we share

After my basketball drills, I walk around the barbed gate

of the neighborhood pool

I climb into the blue green water and float for days

Really I only got an hour before the pool closes

But I don't care when I'm floating

It lets me think

My eyes closed or searching the sky for animal figures

Ice cream cones & airplanes that skip across the blue blue up

The aqua water carry my arms & legs

A body of girl & whoosh

When I'm too tired to move my calves & arms

I climb out the water & feel less rubber band

& more light light

Most days the water burns everything

my nose & eyes & even my hair is too dry

but I feel clean

I feel more me than when I arrived

Lay Li meets me after the pool

She ain't get in the pool but she still wears

her tube top bikini, a towel draped around her shoulder

like a comma.

She bites at her cuticles & I already know

It's been almost two years since silly boys slapped water in the pool

Now the boys are gone & it's just me doing floating like a log

while Mommy & Me classes happen in the shallow end

my muscles hurt after playing Horse alone

A girl on the basketball court ain't no different

than any other baller, if you work hard enough

that's what my cousin Inga say

She the first one to teach me to hold the globe with both hands

to use my right hand to guide the ball.

Finally out of the pool

I can see the harsh water peels my skin

I don't have any cocoa butter on me

So I pull my legs up, crisscross-applesauce

& focus on Lay Li.

When she bites her nails it's not because she's nervous

More like anxious and angry

& always it's about her mama

"So what happened?" I ask

& she frowns at her hands

Then covers her face from the dipping sun

She shrugs

& instantly I feel bad

I know what it feels like to have

Too much to say

So much you can't speak

I make noise when I'm nosy

I slap the mosquitoes gnawing at my legs

It's been a year since we last talked

about her mama but that's the only

thing that bothers her enough

to bite-ruin her perfect nails

But Lay Li don't sweat it

she don't swing at the mosquitoes

she don't even miss a beat.

"That woman been gone so long

I can barely remember what she looks like."

## I CAN'T IMAGINE

what it's like to forget my mother's face

I sit quiet & wait for her story to unfold

My mama still on drugs

& my daddy ain't got time for all that

He don't want us girls to see her like that

He says every child deserve to be the sun

To know they come from the sun

& if the sun snuff itself to dusk before its time

& no shine is left to see

Let it be

One day we woke up & she was already

a cloudy shadow of herself

Then one day we woke up & she was

gone

She only come home when she clean

She only call home when she sorta sober

She ain't never remembered my birthday

or my sisters' birthday & I'm like whatever.

When you live where we live

You say what it is & if you can't say what it is

Or if it hurt too much

Or maybe it's too confusing

You just say "whatever."

That way you ain't no lie

## DON'T NOBODY WANT TO CALL IT

Especially when it got more faces than any solitary name

but if I'm honest

I want to know if Lay Li seen the zombies too

The ones who take over my uncles' bodies

after weeks of playing ghost

only to return him to our front door

with his clothes all crumpled

& eyes brimming red

Lay Li is the only one I can talk to about

The smell of hot ash & burned glass

"You know what it looks like."

She stands up from the grass

swinging her dry striped towel in the air

"It looks like the walking dead."

## ON THE WAY TO MY HOUSE

I need to rinse the chlorine off my skin

I need to remember who I am

Lay Li say, "Where's your cocoa butter?"

& I know she wants to call me ashy.

When I walk through the front door

I'm surprised no one is home

I turn on the television & tell Lay Li I'll be right back

Right out the blue Lay Li calls to me already running up the stairs

"I'm just tired of crying

over someone

that's been gone so long."

## LAY LI LAUGHS

like the joke's on everybody but her

Lay Li

    squints into the mirror & pouts

Lay Li

    applies more lipstick than a little

Lay Li

    takes my lip gloss as backup just in case

Lay Li say

    "It's so boring here. Let's call Shawn."

I laugh like the joke is on Shawn

He's her old crush & first real boyfriend

Since her mama left the house

But then I realized she just called my house boring

& now my feelings are hurt.

Lay Li say

    "Don't be like that. I ain't mean nothing by it."

Lay Li

    pull my ponytail a little

Lay Li

    is forgiven

    again.

## I MOVE

her hand & brush at my hair

I mimic the mirror

Reach to take back my lip gloss

& my pride

from Lay Li's hands

It's the inexpensive kind from the neighborhood CVS

She pretends she's gonna keep it

like a child & its pacifier

her arms swing above both of our heads

helicopter style

Out of my reach

She is pleased with herself

& giggling to my hands

waving in the air

fire the roof is on fire

but it ain't

& I don't crack a smile

This makes her laugh even harder

All her teeth showing

All my steam moving like a cloud when I cut my eyes

She sighs

rolls her eyes

then tosses it to me before she grabs the phone

& dials with one last perfect pink nail

same color as Essa's (I think)

But I don't say anything

Just pucker my lips as

she watches me with boring eyes apply the sheen

Like an impostor.

## SNITCHES

get stitches

So I know how to mind my own business

& make sure I don't tell everybody

the things I know.

It's funny

I ain't realize how much silent sauce I got

Until someone stop talking when Lay Li walk by.

Everything go quiet

Like midnight black

Like static on the TV

Like the sound my mama made that time I asked

"Where is daddy?"

Or like the sound my mama made the time I asked

"What is prison?"

I know what silent sounds like

Lay Li & I haven't talked not once

Since the phone call with Shawn

It's been a whole week

& the argument has grown teeth

Buried its fangs into our friendship

& won't let go.

I tried to shake it loose

Even after she accused me

"You trying to break me & Shawn up?!"

Her and Shawn been on and off all summer

He go to high school on the west side of town

& one of the freshest high tops.

She say "You trying to break me & Shawn up?"

And I think *I want my friend back.*

But not like that

Just want to be able to talk to the only one

who care about how I look when I leave the house

　"Girl, brush your hair"

Just want to be able to talk to the only one

who cares about how I look

　"Lil, give them basketball shorts a break."

Even when she get on my nerves & fix me up with boys

Who can't seem to stand me

The same boys who get mad when I beat them on the court

They say I talk too much mess

I say "Only on the court"

& I ain't no liar, on the court is where it belong

With Lay Li I don't have to think too hard

I'm the friend of the star

& I don't mind, not at all

It gives me time to think about my dreams & the WNBA

But when I call Lay Li & she don't pick up

A pit in my stomach grows like a redwood tree

## A WEEK LATER

& Lay Li still avoid me like the plague

Or a pop quiz

Or a dentist appointment

Or that person who just ate onions for lunch

She don't pick up my calls & now I see her
with Samantha, Octavia, Teeja & Tiffany.

So I start to spend every day after school
at the basketball court doing drills

I think

Maybe today I'll run into Lay Li at the pool

Maybe today she will show up

Maybe today she won't be mad at me anymore

Maybe today she treat me better than dirt

I only get sad when I round the corner & see only

the Mommy & Me group is in the pool

I pull off my basketball shorts
& tug the straps of my stupid swimsuit

before I dive into the deep end.

## THE NEXT DAY AT SCHOOL

I'm mad

Essa got on my nerves the night before

& made a joke about me not having no friends

"Look at Lay Li," she said. "Even she don't want to be around you!"

Today, I sit around the taco bar

near the far side of the lunchroom

& remember all the places I can easily disappear into.

1. Sit by the bench under the tree by the bus stop

Sit next to the girl with her brand-new bra gleaming
in the locker room

& I can hear everybody lying to each other.

I sip on my Capri-Sun

& remember what happens

when everyone talks around me

like no one is listening.

2. Sit by the hopscotch outline on the concrete

by the house

### 3. Sit by the stairs near the attendance office

I hear them say

I sip tea

I say

I mind my own

But everything is everything when you are just who you are

No one special enough to cause a stir

No one who would cause boys to break their necks

I ain't mad that I don't stand out

I just know I've never stood out before.

When I was younger, I thought I had superpowers

Thought if I sat real still and stared at a book

No one would be able to see me

I got so good at it

I forget that I'm the only one playing the game

Sit still with a book or my head down & you can go missing

& just like that

Everybody talks so much around me

It's like I ain't even there

Sometimes

I forget I'm there too

that's how I hear too much information

that's how I learn all the things I didn't know

I want to know.

My lunch of hard shell tacos turns to mush in my hands

Just like me

They can't hold on to everything anymore

I'm tired of chasing people to be my friend

In my head I can still hear her when we argued

"You ruined everything"

"You ruined everything"

"You ruined everything"

I'm tired of being worried about people not liking me

I can't do it anymore

I can't let Essa get under my skin

I can't let my opponents on the court make me feel
like I don't belong

I don't even want these damn tacos anymore


I drop my tray in the trash & head out the door

## BASKETBALL DRILLS #2

My sister, Essa,

is the smart one

I shoot *swish*

But she also lies so much

I think it's her favorite song

I shoot *swish*

She lies so much she never know when the truth sneaks up

I shoot

She lies so much it sound like a history lesson

*miss*

She lies so much she'll make you believe rain is a color
coming out the sky

I shoot

& when she lies like she do

I still think she makes rainbows

*miss*

Because no one forgets her name.

I shoot

*backboard bounce swish*

Everywhere she goes they laugh at all her jokes

Everywhere she goes they call her brilliant

Everywhere she goes they also call her slick talker

I shoot *miss* shoot *miss* shoot *bricks*

Essa lies so much she never knows when the truth sneaks up

& smack her in the mouth!

shoot: *swish*

(That's what our grandma Maxi say)

& I think it's hilarious

I laugh & laugh & laugh

   with all my teeth showing

shoot: *swish*

except Grandma Maxi don't play that

   "kids laughing at grown folks' jokes."

So

S H O O T M Y S H O T

I grin real big

   with my lips shut

     t i g h t . . .

(*swish*)

## ON THE WEEKEND, I GO TO THE MALL WITH ESSA & INGA

Did I tell you how much Essa hates me?
(It's like her & Lay Li got more in common each day!)

Lucky for me our cousin Inga is around
The house like the big hand on the clock
So what Inga say *goes* & she always comes
through for me

Right on time

Even though Essa tell me she can't stand me
& to get my own friends

I pull on my crisp new Chucks
& cover up my crop-top basketball camp shirt

We walk to the front yard where Inga's mama
Auntie Renee's car is parked

It's an old dusty white Cutlass
It looks like a cloud
It looks like a dream

Essa starts capping hard

On the car being so old

Jesus prolly used dinosaur bones for petro

But Inga pays her no mind

She checks the rearview mirror

& looks at Essa with her eyes stone cold

"Shut up before I make you walk"

& I cackle a little too loud

Because Essa snaps her head around like an owl

"What you laughing at? If I walk, then you walk!"

I close my mouth & pull the hoodie over my bangs.

# WE PULL INTO THE PARKING LOT

& everybody & their mama is here

Nannies & grandmamas & strollers & loud babies wailing

Teenagers with their scooters & three-wheelers

Helmets that match their checkered Vans

Girls from the private school in their mandatory uniforms

Folded up above the knee sit against the entryway

& watch the coordinated chaos

Lay Li had to stay home

Her dad don't play that go out & leave your siblings mess

So I'm stuck with my sister, Essa, (who hates me)

& our cousin Inga (who loves me)

Inga walks through the double doors like a queen

& I pull my hoodie off my head so I can see her clearly

She commands attention when she walks into a room

Her bun wrapped tightly in a knot at the top of her head

Her leggings & knee-high boots match her fanny pack

Slung effortlessly across her shoulder.

Essa also moves like royalty

Her head upright & her shoulders squared

When she isn't angry with me

She beams like her dimples are a gift to the world.

I walk behind them both in awe & inspired

I straighten my shoulders

Paste a smile on my face

I'm more happy inside than I am on the outside

But I feel like this is what I should do

Even though I'm wearing my old cut-out jeans

It feels good to walk with my family

& not have to worry about if they like me or not

& when I think it can't get no better

Inga turns around after we pass the pretzel spot

In the food court & winks

"I think you got a fan, Lil' Cousin."

## SHE POINTS TO THE GROUP

Of guys sitting on a bench

with her short & shiny manicured nails

& before I can figure out who she's talking about

The tallest one from the bunch moves forward.

He is wearing a pair of camouflage cargo pants

& flannel patterned shirt

His hat covers his brown eyes

But I can tell he's looking right at me

He walks away from the group

& I see some of the boys from the court

Today they look at me different

It must be the outfit.

He walks closer to me

Five foot eleven

His hands in his pockets

I think my heart could fit in his hands

He smiles a little

& I decide I could like him

"What's up? I'm Clifton," he says.


His eyes never move from my face

& it's so intense

 It's like I'm in the pool again

  Underwater

  Holding my breath

  My arms are floating

  Away from my body


I'm in the mall now

 But in my head

  I'm in the pool after practice

  & I get the same calming feeling I get

  When I jump into the deep end blue

  & sink until I rise again

  Left arm

  Right leg kick

  Right arm

Left leg kick

Butterfly

Till both arms lift out the sorta sea together

But I'm not in the pool

I remind myself

But in my chest

I begin to backstroke

to open my eyes & check out the sky

I wade in the teal azul when a fire burns my chest

Even in the cold pool, I know I must be careful

I don't want to sink

If I'm not careful

like now

I could lose my breath

## MY FIRST TIME OUT WITH CLIFTON

I know the world is going to end.

Mama don't play that

"company over when grown folks out the house" business

& even though Essa is home with cousin Inga

they ain't grown:

They're just teenagers

With a curfew that ain't dictated by the sun

going down & the streetlights coming on

They're just teenagers

Who curse when the neighbors are looking

But never when they own parents are looking cause

They ain't got a death wish

They're just teenagers

With a taste for the kind of freedom

They've only seen on sitcoms

The kind with two-parent households

not homes like ours

More like Inga's mom, Auntie Renee, who saves coupons

& works every day, clockwork ready for the water company

More like Inga's mom, Auntie Renee, who on her day off

will drive by different houses with FOR SALE signs

plastered in their yard, with her eyes bright & dancing

singing Luther Vandross to whoever is in the passenger seat

More like Mama, who tells me to ignore Essa's attitude

Cause she works too many hours & ain't got time

To listen to our argument when she finally come home.

More like Mama, who calls me her baby
(mostly cause I am the last born)

Who works too many hours to make it to my basketball games

& the house better be clean cause you don't want to get

on her bad side

More like Mama, the sweetest woman I've ever known

Who still got rules that we betta follow cause ain't nobody

in this house more grown than her.

## THE RULES ARE EASY

No boys in the house when I'm gone

Nobody who don't live here in the house when I'm gone

    (Who left on the light?)

    (Who do you think you are?)

Nobody mess up the kitchen before I get home to cook

Nobody eat all the cereal

Nobody eat all the bread

Nobody go begging for food like we're poor

    (You trying to make me look like a bad parent?)

    (You acting like you don't know no better?)

No, you can't go over to that house

Yes, you can go to the park

Be back before dark

    (Nobody walked the dog?)

    (Nobody folded the clothes?)

    (Who do you think I am?)

    (I work all day and got to come home and work too?)

No fighting in the house

No running from fights

That school better not call my phone

Don't steal snacks from the store—we ain't broke

Make ramen for snack

Make a peanut-butter sandwich

Don't use all my butter

Don't eat all the cheese

Take the chicken out the freezer

   (Ain't nobody take the chicken out the freezer?)

Nobody call my phone unless the house is on fire

Watch your mouth

   (Who do you think you're talking to?)

I'm not one of your little friends.

## SO, WHEN CLIFTON ASKS TO USE THE BATHROOM

after we walk home from the basketball game

I forget about Mama's rule.

I am too busy thinking

about the cold shoulder

Lay Li tossed my way

It's been weeks since she & I talked.

But it feels like eternity

When I see Lay Li sitting like the bleachers are her throne

I can still hear her voice in my head "You ruin everything!"

I walk in the orange-lit gymnasium

with my mall purchase, a pair of hot pink stretch pants

& I got a date (with a boy from a different school)

all on my own

But Lay Li ain't even speak

& I thought for sure she'd be impressed.

I thought:

Here I go

just shining

like my own

s u n .

## HERE I GO

beaming

with somebody
Lay Li ain't had to trick into pretending to like me

& Lay Li acts like it's nothing

Like I'm nothing.

All because I didn't lie to Shawn

who likes her too much

& keep on asking me questions.

## SHAWN WANTS TO KNOW ABOUT CURTIS


& why Lay Li & him broke up

in the first place

He doesn't believe she left Curtis for him

He doesn't believe much of what she say

Because word is out that Curtis is her first everything

First real boyfriend

First real love

First real kiss

First hand to touch her like the slow songs sing about

Now, nobody calls Curtis a lie

It don't matter if he got caught in a lie

It don't matter if he forget the first story he told

It don't matter if he never answers the questions outright

He just nod & shrug & the boys say

*I knew it!*

& everybody think they know

& mostly they don't

But the truth don't matter

when you got better stories to tell yourself

Now,

Shawn runs the West Side

& Curtis runs the South Side

Both sides hold court during away sports games

Where the most popular guys

Talk this & that

Brag about girls they bagged

The new kicks they got

The game they watched on television

The summer school they going to for summer

Who got smoked

Who got smoke

Who smoke

They talk as much as they say us girls do

& still they never say much


Lay Li say whether or not

Lay Li & Curtis hooked up

It ain't nobody's business

& I agree

## BUT CURTIS LET IT BE EVERYBODY'S BUSINESS

& that's how they broke up.

Lay Li decides

Finger *snap*: just like that

"Curtis never existed. He never happened. Never speak his name."

I say "Okay." Okay.
But when Shawn asks if they ever really hooked up, I say

"Curtis is a dog!" instead of "Ask Lay Li."

Which really feels like the same thing

Except it ain't.

One says "I'll lie for my friend."

& other proves I will try

to lie for my friend

& fail.

Just like that: finger *snap* Lay Li decides I don't exist too.

She's talking into the phone until Shawn hangs up.

She calls back.

He won't answer.

She calls again

She calls me jealous.

He won't answer.

The ring is the loudest ring that never ends

Before she slams the phone on the table

Before she cries in her hands

Before I realize I've never seen her like this

Her makeup smeared & running a river into the brink
of her palms

She picks up the phone & calls Shawn

No Answer

She calls Shawn again

No Answer

She turns to cry on my shoulder

For a moment, I exist again

My hand on her back patting softly in Morse code

I'm sorry I'm sorry It will be okay

"Maybe I can call him back?"

I ask

My mind racing trying to fix what I didn't know was broken

But Lay Li stops crying

Wipes her face on her sleeve & looks me dead in my eyes

I don't exist.

I don't exist.

I don't

## I AIN'T NEVER BEEN GOOD AT LYING

To: Lay Li

I'm sorry

I didn't mean to

But I ain't never been a good liar

Mama told me so

She say

You got a way of repeating back a question
until it sounds old & worn

Like shoes with bad soles

& no one can believe a story

with all them pauses

## ANYWAYS, LIKE I WAS SAYING

I walk in the gym with Clifton

He    two steps behind me—all lanky & lean

He    make me feel pretty

He    see me in a way I never thought
    I wanted eyes to look at me before.

He    looks at me
    like the boys look at Lay Li

So I thought she'd understand when Clifton & I walked in together.

Cheerleaders strut by in their orange & green outfits

the tassels & orange pom-poms

are small & flurry globes & bounce like sparklers

to anyone with enough patience

to look closely.

This the part where Clifton look at me real close

I stop walking

My mouth wide open

He says "Your eyes are like diamonds"

& I want to smile.

## BUT I KNOW BAD GAME WHEN I HEAR IT

Especially when the entire fourth grade in Ms. Meeks's class
worked these same tired similes

The thing is

Clifton said it to ME

& he don't know what I worked on
during fourth-grade English

Or how I walk the halls & everyone make fun of me.

The thing about bullies is

They only notice the people that don't fight back

They take your kindness for weakness

But I'm not weak
I'm just tired of swinging

## WHEN KIDS HAVE

a different daddy than their siblings
It's hard to remember what comes first
The heart hurt or the stomach growl.

Essa got a different daddy
He's okay
Not mean, like her

But my dad is a ghost.

Mama say
Some people can't stay out of jail

Essa say
He ain't never want you

    her nails click in the air like they closing a casket

Cousin Inga say
Essa just jealous

But I know hate when I see it.

# AFTER FOURTH GRADE

I learned "You think you so smart" is a threat

In high school, without no daddy to show me how to dribble

Or pivot

With a sister who act like she hate me

& a cousin who more sister than cousin

I figure, I'm safer if I stay away from light

Ain't no daddy to say move right, right left

Mama work for everyone, so I don't hold my breath

Just stay away from the spotlight

The light gets too hot for brown girls like me to feel safe.

This is when I learned to play not as smart

This is when I learned to keep my hands

in my lap during Mr. Wacobi's class

This is when I learned to not run as fast

This is when I stop beating the boys

in running

& kickball

& tetherball

& T-ball

This is how I learn to play not as big

cause nobody got time for a girl outshining them.

## MY BIG COUSIN INGA ASKS ME

"Who you playing small for?"

& I pretend I don't know what she's talking about

She's five foot eleven & the tallest woman in our family

She's a basketball coach for the lil' kid league during summer

& after she saw I had handles in fourth grade

she ain't let me drop the rock since

"Who you playing small for?"

Means:

I don't get to slink into the corner.

I don't get to find a home in the shadow.

Not when there is a court nearby.

Inga attends Downtown Community College

& talks to Essa almost every day

But sometimes it's like they don't even like each other.

When Essa & Inga's arguments get too big

& Essa screams into the phone

Then it's weeks before I see Inga again

I'll come home from the pool & she'll be

on the porch or sitting on the hood of her mama's car

waiting for Essa to come home from her classes at State

She'll shrug when I say where you been & then say

"I love her, but I don't like her. Most times, I think if

We weren't related, we wouldn't be around each other at all."


When she's at the house, we go straight to the court

She makes me play her one-on-one

She hits the ball out my hand if I'm sloppy


She kicks at my feet planted

& shakes her head

"Play D! Lil'—what did I teach you?!"


Inga calling me Lil' tells me I'm someone's sister

Inga calling me Lil' shows me I'm not out here on my own

& everything I do means something to someone else


& just like that I begin to play for keeps.

On the court

There is no mercy

I'm a baller

& I don't care who is bothered by all the space

I take up.

## SO, WHEN CLIFTON SAYS

that sweet sweet simile

from fourth-grade English

I force a smile

I hold his hand

& look past the bleachers for Lay Li.

The day I met Clifton at the mall

Was the day I wore my cousin Tia's hoodie

From the thrift store

& Inga flat-ironed my hair real cute

& my bangs fell all around the front of my face

& Essa rolled her eyes at me

So I know I was fly.

## PAST THE BLEACHERS

In the corner

Next to the far side of the green gym doors

Lay Li sits like the queen

surrounded by some girls from Fashion Club

They all wear their tight yellow pants

They all shine bright

   like diamonds.

Lay Li see me

& usually she would wave me over

tell whatever girl on her right side to move over.

"She's my right hand."

But not today

   We just stare each other down.

## SHE LOOKS ME HARD IN MY EYES

& my knees lock into tree trunks

My eyes don't dance like my heartbeat racing

They stare straight back hot daggers.

I remember things will never be the same.

I remember things

## WILL NEVER BE THE SAME

I got my own ideas

I got my own body

I got my own mind.

I let Clifton lead me to the bleachers

on the opposite side of the court.

I realize as I plop down

on the bleacher seats

ain't no one but my mama

& Lay Li

ever held my hand before.

## THERE IS A RUMOR GOING AROUND

& I know it got my name on it.

That's how Tre got shot

That's how Teneisha got got

Rumors be the worst thing since government cheese.

Grandma Maxi say:

"Hands crisscrossed across the chest

mean you got something to hide."

She also say "make a cheese sandwich for after-school snack"

No matter the stomachache that come for me.

Let Teneisha tell it

Keeping to yourself won't save you

She was just at the bus stop

& the girls jumped her for wearing blue

& the girls jumped her for talking

to their boyfriends at the Mack Road mall

& the girls jumped her because she think she cute

& I don't want my name attached to a beatdown

Or a rumor

But laws of the school say I got at least one (if not both)

coming to me.

## I FIGURE IT'S THE RUMOR

Cause it gets too quiet

When I walk into a room

Like even my breath is being judged

& my whole stomach turns on itself

tight & rock hard

like I just ate one of them cheese sandwiches

I wish I could ask Lay Li what happened.

Why is everyone staring at me?

But I got too many questions

& not one person to depend on for answers.

## WHEN A RUMOR HIT THE WIND


The room is a graveyard of friends

These the same girls that laugh when I laugh

But now they laugh without including me

Now they take pictures with each other

& I ain't nowhere in the frame.

## HAVE YOU EVER STARTED A RUMOR?


Like not on purpose

Maybe you shared a secret

& the secret got wings

& then someone shared that

Same secret with wings except

They gave it a candle

Cause it was too dark or something

Maybe they needed some light

& maybe the wings took flight

With the light & maybe they

Shared that same candle winged thing

With someone that don't know or don't care

& in the wind that flame goes

Lighting up all the dead

Do you know

how it can start

slow like a burn

or a tickle

until it's not funny anymore?

it feels like a needle

pressing down

before the nurse gives the vaccination shot

it feels like a joke

that everyone is laughing at

except the person

they're joking about

instead of laughing

that warm glow that grows

inside your chest & hands

& crawls across your cheeks

like some uncontrollable kind of happy

it feels more like

closing your eyes

tight

so tight

the air can't get in

& the water can't get out

can you feel the sting?

that's how it feels

like a forever

sting.

## WHEN I'M ON THE BASKETBALL COURT

I ain't laughed at

I ain't pointed at

I ain't forgotten

I ain't really myself at all

The only place that feel as good as the court

Is when I'm in Clifton's arms

In his arms I ain't laughed at

In his arms I ain't pointed at

In his arms I ain't forgotten

With Clifton I feel like I'm on the court

My heart is certain

His hands frame my face

Like my hands hold the rock

His lips come to mine

& my heart flutter the same

As when I realize the ball into the air

The net waving a welcome song

Perfect aim

No *swish*

My first kiss? *I Swoon*

When I'm on the court.

## IT'S TOO HOT TO THINK ABOUT THINKING

I had my first (but third in life) kiss

With Clifton & no one to talk to about it

Lay Li looked at me & I looked back

Like that

Everything is dust

But now that it's Saturday

& all my chores are done

I have nothing better to do.

I have no one to turn to

I make my way around the corner

Maybe I can play pickup

I bop across the grass &

As soon as my ten toes touch asphalt

all the boys groan

It's too hot to think about thinking

We play three-on-three

My team ain't trash but my mind is everywhere.

I miss an assist

I miss my free throw

I'm fouled & I keep quiet.

Not like me.


The sweat pours from my pores

The game of twenty-one is just beginning.

Tyrone & the rest of the boys

from the summer program

let me play but never in peace.

My handles

I swerve

Ankles intact

Don't travel

Dribble

Dribble

Pump fake

Tyrone falls for it

Swings his arms for the story

No glory

Just a clean shot

Look at my elbow

Ain't it just a shelf for a bottle of your tears

*Score*

Tyrone fouls me again

This time I'm fouled & I am foul.

I point my finger at his basketball shorts

Call his game as raggedy as his clothes

# THE ASPHALT IS HOT ON MY SNEAKERS


but it's too hot to think

& I can't care about them stupid boys not wanting me to play


Cause they can't beat me.

That's why they mad

That's why Tyrone suck his teeth

That's why he pushes me when I get the ball in my possession.

But I still talk tough

Just like Inga taught me


My mouth so mine

It cut rocks into pebbles

It cut glass into shatter

It cut metal into sharp silver slices


I even talk smack to Coach Willie

When I'm on the court it's different

The rules are different

& ain't no jail

& no Mama to worry about disappointing

I am my own on the blacktop

But the blacktop ain't where folks keep their feelings

So when Tyrone pushed me into the closet last year

& Coach Willie let him

I realize a girl's mouth is a weapon

I realize the game is fixed


When I play ball, they say my mouth too big

Coach Willie, our summer camp counselor,

Say "I got the nerve to talk like a boy"

He say I ain't supposed to say them things.

Not with my girl mouth

& I was almost surprised

Cause I ain't said nothing that they haven't already said to me.

& with all my tough talk, I still don't talk about nobody's mama

Cause Tyrone's mama reminds me of my uncle

   Sick on that stuff

& I don't talk about his daddy neither

   Cause his daddy gone just like mines.

Instead

I say      "Your handles is trash!"


& really, that's only a fact.

## TYRONE MAD CAUSE IT'S TRUE

His face turns dark around the eyes

His lips purse into a curse word

& he pushes me against the backboard bar

& he pushes my head

& he tries to take the ball out my hands.

But I already told you

I'm too quick

I know how to deal with these kind of boys

The kind that don't keep they hands to themselves.

I pivot fast on my right

I drop my hip & push all my weight on the same heel

My left foot crunches into his size eleven shoes

My whole body crashes up & then back

I try to push his lower body through his stomach

I try to push through his nightmares

I want to remind him to never touch me again

I send him thrashing to the dirty concrete

Then I sit the ball down by his body squirming

& walk away slow.

## I'M STILL MAD

when I walk up the block around the corner

away from Tyrone

I am steaming mad

I am

So mad I can't hear Clifton calling my name.

He jogs from the bus stop up the hill above the playground

& right towards me

It's like my blood is boiling

& my heart is racing

& my eyes see rain

But it's burning up outside.

I stretch my extra T-shirt across my shoulders

I count backwards from ten

& try to remember what Cousin Inga said:

"don't play small"

On repeat.

It's so loud in my head

I never hear Clifton calling my name

from the edge of the basketball court

his eyes shaded by his hands

It's too loud.

It's too loud.

My ears ringing from the noise in my blood.

## I DON'T REALIZE I'M ON THE PORCH OF LAY LI'S HOUSE

Until I ring the doorbell & sit on the porch steps

Her house is closer to the ball court

But far away enough for me to gather my thoughts

Especially in this heat.

I want to go swimming

I want to forget about the court for a minute.

Lay Li's little sisters come outside without saying a word

I know Lay Li sent them.

*"Hi,"* they say in chorus

Both of their pigtails bouncing with plastic BoBo's at the ends

Of their thick braided hair

*"Hi,"* I say weakly & try to smile

Then look at my reflection in their glass screen door

My messy ponytail

& my basketball shorts rumpled.

The older of the twin sisters ask: *"What happened?"*

& I give her a frown as my answer: *nothing*.

We sit there in silence for one whole minute

Before a group of kids riding by on their bikes

Catch my attention.

Their hands up in the air

Their weight balanced on the black seat

They are laughing like I used to laugh with Lay Li

& I remember Lay Li & me ain't really

Got nothing to say no more.

I don't know why.

I just know it is what it is.

I just know we ain't friends no more.

## I FINALLY STAND UP

& younger twin says "Lay Li said she be out in a minute"

But I shrug & say "Never mind."

& bounce up the block

toward the street where my house sits alone

Without ever looking back.

## I JUST WANT TO TELL LAY LI

about my kiss with Clifton

He is almost a whole five inches taller than me

I figure this out as I count three whole "Mississippi"s

before his lips reach mine.

This will be my third kiss.

But the first one doesn't count.

See that's where Lay Li comes in

& that's why it's important that she knows

What happens next

Because my quote-unquote first kiss

happened in a closet

In the dark

With everyone outside the door

Waiting to hear how it went.

The game was called "Seconds in Heaven"

& I ain't really even want to play

   But Lay Li said: "Don't be a child."

## LAY LI GOT A WAY

of sounding way older than she is

which makes anyone on the other side of her advice

feel stupid or even worse, young & stupid.

Lay Li was held back a year in middle school.

She say it was right when her mama went off the deep

end & she had to raise her younger sisters, Liz & Leah,

before her daddy stepped in.

One day after school

I watched her washing mismatched plates & cereal bowls

little trails of her younger sisters' breakfast left in the sink

her eyes never blinked but she almost smiled.

Her given name is Liliane

But she say "My mama gave me that name

& I don't keep nothing that woman gave me."

## LAY LI SAYS GOOGLE MAKES

everything perfect

Look it up:

How do you fix a run in your stocking?

    You don't.

How do you make a boy fall in deep like?

    Focus on your lip gloss

    Always apply a second coat

    Touch his arm whenever you can

    Don't let him grab you up

How to kiss?

    Find a mirror

    Purse your lips together

    Kiss the glass

    Make sure it isn't wet when you pull back

    & stare at the impression of your breath

    Do it again

How to fight the sadness?

Dance to your favorite song loud loud

Call your friends & talk them into walking the mall with you

Call someone that likes you more than you like them

   & let their adoration fill you up

Put on your favorite pair of leggings

   & strut to the corner store slow

Buy something small:

   a pack of gum, a candy bar, or a bag of Flamin' Hot Cheetos

Laugh loud in front of your enemies

Don't write about it       *Don't write about it?*

Nah, don't leave evidence of the sads.

& never ever let it take you somewhere you can't come back from.

## NOW, WHEN I GET A CHANCE TO HAVE MY FIRST KISS

I jump

Literally

Out my skin

Then I climb in the closet with Adrian from the junior class.

The thing is my shorts ain't short enough

& my tank top ain't tight at all

I figure I ain't too much to look at no way

So, when Adrian

choose me for a round of "Seconds in Heaven"

I decide he know what to do with a kiss

Besides

He got the freshest flattop

& run the Edison Alternative School

the one opposite RFK Prep Academy up the hill

You know,

The one we heard all the bad stories about.

## STORIES

like the ceiling with water falling in on the classrooms
even after it rains for days on end. The desks are moved to the
front of the room leaving the blue wastebaskets to collect the water
before one of the students is assigned with dumping
the water in the nearest bathroom sink.

who compare videos of girls in their locker rooms. Like the boys who leak the videos online when they mad. Like the boys who leak the videos online when they get bored. How the videos made the girl into a mess her mother would have to clean up. Like the time the mother transferred the girl out of school because her daughter couldn't walk into a room without people whispering & giggling. Like the boys were expelled from the entire school district. Like the girl went to a whole other school & by the time she got there the videos had surfaced over there too. Like the boys never really felt no kind of way because they were too busy being celebrated & given high fives from their homies.

## STORIES LIKE THE ONES WE HEARD ABOUT ANGEL

She was once the one everyone wanted to be like.
Until Lay Li arrived on campus. Tight jeans with patches

strategically placed everywhere: Hip. Butt. Right knee.
Left shin. It made the eyes check out her fly. Her baby hair

was eco style perfect and her lips pouted with the shiniest
MAC sheen ever. I didn't really hang with Angel then.

But I thought she was nice enough. We all dance in a circle
at homecoming one year when we still thought

a bunch of barrettes and a set of earrings made you
special enough to be remembered.

Angel had light light eyes. Like green, light. Like tree,
bright. She sport her ash-blond hair

bone straight. Which was pretty hard to do
surrounded by all the valley's humidity. But Angel

ain't gave up. She kept a brown brush in her back
pocket & tied the handle with her green scrunchie.

Angel had four younger siblings. All of them
heads full of ash-blond hair. Curly tight bangs

covered their eyes like a perfect Disney character.
But they mama being the janitor at our grade school

made them the butt of everyone's jokes. I ain't laugh.
Ain't nothing funny about making sure your kids fed.

But Angel couldn't get away from the laughter.

## STORIES ABOUT ANGEL'S MAMA

began to circulate like a wasp's nest, bothered.
Someone said they socks went missing.

Someone said they lunch money went missing.
Everyone blamed Angel's mama. Sat in her face

in the lunchroom and dared her to pounce.
But Angel was sugar sweet. At first,

she didn't like to fight. Rumor has it
her daddy beat her mama. That's why

her mama walked slow around the rooms,
cleaning & humming. No hurry. No care

for the things that children might say
about her. Just feeling like she had to get

from one task to the next, safely.
One day, it's like Angel woke up.

Just wound up her fists & started swinging.

Some think maybe she started to fight
so people would stop focusing on her mama.

But Angel's anger grew
until it had legs,
arms,
and its own nervous system.

She stole a car once.
She fought on the back of the bus another time.

She smacked a girl over lollipops
in the back of the team van.
As it drove the cheerleaders
to the away game
across town.

## STORIES CAN CHANGE WHO YOU ARE TO YOURSELF

*Shoot,* stories can change your whole world. Look at Angel. Darius became her world. & here comes a whole new story about who Angel is & how we will remember her. Darius became a new story. He was an older boy at Burbank High that took a real liking to her. Saw her at one of the away games & told her to sit beside him after the game was finished. He wasn't a ballplayer. But he was respected. Black hoodie and army fatigue jacket covered his shoulders. And he didn't smile much. But when he saw her, he did. In no time Angel and Darius were inseparable. People stopped talking bad about Angel's mama. But Angel ain't stop swinging. Angel quit cheerleading altogether. Darius was known to be hot tempered and even more hot handed. He swung on anybody. He connects like Iron Fist. Like Street Fighter. Like Mortal Kombat. Him & Angel began to turn on each other. It got to the point Angel ain't allowed to walk too far away from Darius when she visits him at the away games. My mama said that's a bad recipe. & the way her & my pops broke up, I believe her. Boys from other schools who don't know what's the what. History ain't always passed easily. And Angel is beautiful like that. She caused boys to stop and talk about silly things. Talk about anything that would keep her attention. Darius get to swinging on the boy that look too long into her pretty eyes. He doesn't listen to Angel screams, telling him to stop. He tried to swing on her school security too. That's how he got kicked out of Burbank and afterward the only school that would take him is Edison Alternative. At least that's the story I heard.

## BUT I THINK MY STORY ABOUT MY FIRST KISS

begins here.

With Adrian & me facing each other

In a closet.

Adrian smells like fresh-cut grass & hay

It makes my nose itch

But at least he looks at me

& not through me.

I'm so used to people looking through me to get to Lay Li.

I don't even realize it.

I just know my nose itches

& my palms are sweaty

& he is looking at me

His hand on my shoulder

My hand on his knee

I try to keep still to ignore the itch of my nose

But it takes my attention & won't let go

My stomach swirls & dips

that's got to mean something.

## THE THING

about a kiss is:

    if it's too wet

    it's the worst

    & if it's too dry

    it hurts.

I learned these rules reading my grandma's
Harlequin romance novels.

Someone always graces the cover in a ball gown
with the moonlight peeking from behind a castle or something

The woman's arms are almost always wrapped tight
like a scarf around a rich-looking white man's neck

Both their eyes closed    lips locked    & looking
some kind of sleep.

## IN THE CLOSET I SIT & WAIT FOR ADRIAN

to close his eyes

like the romance book cover

like the movie *Pretty Woman.*

But he doesn't

He looks

right

at

me

Eyes not blinking or nothing

Mouth hanging open like a barn door

& he leans in quick

Except I'm quick

## TOO

Too quick

I put my head down
& give him a headbutt to the nose.

Red violet spills open everywhere.

The closet begins to smell like pennies in a wet fist
& before I can blink
The door is flung open
Adrian is tumbling out with his paws over his flooded face.

Everyone is laughing
Everyone except Lay Li.

I guess it's cause she knows this means:
she has more work to do.

Except I ain't never asked for her help
Just asked for her to be my friend.

## HERE COME THE SENIOR BOYS

from Burbank High School

It's been ten days since I found myself on Lay Li's porch,

waiting

I found myself lost

This is what I remember now

Sitting by myself at an away game

Clifton on the other side of the gym with his friends

Me by myself with my memories

## REMEMBER WHEN?

Lay Li said to no one in particular.

"Why she always looking at me?"

& I looked around to see who she was talking about.

"Who?"

Lay Li blinks at me slow

like I'm stupid

like she can't believe I asked such a dumb question

Lay Li blinks slow like the red hand warning

"STOP"

& then responds

"Angel! Look at her. She always staring

at me like she want smoke!"

& I nod like I agree & I have all the answers.

## REMEMBER WHEN I DIDN'T HAVE THE ANSWER?

but I pretended real quick
"I don't know what she's looking at!"
My eyes shoot daggers defending Lay Li
& Angel's eyes go down down down
to her shoes
      shell-toed sneakers with the label
faded & holding her jeans like a prayer.

Angel's smile goes down down down
to the pit of her stomach like      nightfall
like the room is spinning & she might be sick.

Then I feel sick

Because here I am with a chance to do different

& instead of being loyal to myself

I rather be loyal to Lay Li.
My mama say I got a mean mug

when things ain't going my way

& I perfected it for moments just like this

To protect my friends

It's what I wear when I walk home alone

It's what I wear when I'm on the court playing ball

It's what I wear when Essa talk slick & now

It's what I wear when Lay Li say someone is bothering her.

Angel walks past

The boys can't help but turn they heads.

Like Lay Li she's pretty

But unlike Lay Li, she act like she don't know it.

## REMEMBER WHEN LAY LI SAID

"If you see something you like

You got to pretend you don't like it so much"?

& I tried on her swag

I walked around the mall full of its see-through things

Sort of looking at boys

Sort of looking at shoes

Both of these I can't afford.

I don't trip

Until the air changed

& right ahead of us stands Angel

surrounded by a flock of dudes.

She's laughing in her crop top & acid-washed jeans.

We catch her eye

& Angel smiles in my direction.

Angel got pretty eyes & wear her ponytail to the side

Lay Li suck her teeth

Stuff her hands in her back pocket & turn on

her heel digs into the marble floor

her back to Angel's eager glance.

## I REMEMBER WHEN IT ALL CHANGED

This was weeks before the Shawn incident

But after I proved I was willing to be mean to a girl

That ain't never did nothing to me

Me & Lay Li were hanging out at my house
when Essa came home

I was trying on outfits
& Lay Li sat on the edge of the bed grimacing

"No"

"Absolutely not"

& "Damn! You ain't got anything else?
Besides those ugly basketball shorts?"

Essa stood at the doorway & laughed a laugh
that shook the walls before she said

"She's so corny! She ain't got nothing that I ain't give her."

& Essa was right.
Most of my clothes were hand-me-downs from her
or summer basketball T-shirts with the sleeves cut off.

Essa & Lay Li laughed     & laughed     & laughed

    & laughed   &    laughed   &   l a u g h e d

So long the hairs on my arm stood up     electric

The air sizzled & a levee behind my eyes broke

Rivers & streams stream down my face     I face them both

& before I can speak Essa tosses her hand in the air.

"You're such a crybaby. We were only playing, dang."

I bend over to throw my clothes in a pile
in the corner of the room

& change my mind

Lay Li isn't laughing anymore

But she ain't speaking either

As I pick up an armful of clothes I toss them at Essa's face

I don't realize until it's too late that a sneaker is in the pile

Until she's howling & holding her eye with one hand

Lay Li never said sorry

Lay Li never said sorry

When I finally look in the mirror to wash my face

I don't even recognize my reflection

Black streaks & smeared lip gloss

With a black scowl cover my face

Lay Li never said sorry

Lay Li never said sorry

She just ran to the kitchen to help Essa with ice for her
blackening eye

## HERE COME THE VALLEY HIGH BOYS

As Clifton & his friends hoot for the hoopers

He sees me staring at him a couple of rows away

& walks over to me. "You okay?" he asks.

& I smile because my voice is somewhere

Far away tucked deep inside my yesterdays.

"Come over here." He grabs my hand & guides me to

A new day.

Which is really just another set of bleachers

With girls waiting for their boyfriends to return

To their side & pay them some attention

I don't mind. I guess I'm used to the background

I don't mind. I need some time to think.

All the things floating in my head keep me dizzy

Off centered I lean both elbows on my legs

& breathe deep

"Hey, you okay?"

I don't realize how far I am from now

I look to my left, head still in the cup of my hands

& see Kiyana for the first time

She sits there staring at me worried

"You don't look so good, are you okay?"

I nod. I nod.

I sit up & clear my throat

"I'm good. I'm good. Thanks."

"My name is Kiyana. I think you play ball with my brother,

Andre. Right?"

## AFTER THE BALL GAME, I REALIZE

Kiyana & me got a lot in common:

We talk sports

Being the only girl around boys

(Andre is her twin brother & they're the youngest of five)

But she doesn't play ball, she's an artist

She talks about painting with the same intensity

As I play ball.

Her Basquiat shirt is faded & torn at the neckline

She has an oversized faded bomber jacket with

A Raiders crest on the sleeve

Tyrone walks up & rolls his eyes at me

Tries to get her attention with "Hey, Kiyana,

When you gonna call me?"

She turns her head away from him

& eyes the exit sign, not mean

But not interested

"Never, Tyrone."

I like her style.

## BASKETBALL DRILLS #3

both hands grip the orange world

ridges in black talk back to my fingertips

I try to worry about my aim

But all I can think about is what I got & what I lost

Clifton

  Lay Li

Clifton

  Lay Li

Clifton

  Lay Li

Clifton Clifton Lay Li

   Clifton Clifton Clifton

Lay Li

Clifton

Clifton?

## CLIFTON & I FALL OFF

First, he's upset that I talk to Kiyana during the game

Then he's upset that I don't want to hang out at the all-night
diner when he knows I got curfew

Then he's upset because he asked me to skip playing ball
& I pretended like I ain't hear him

& now a week later & neither of us call each other.

It's been a month of us hanging out
& I'm already overwhelmed with
whatever this is

There are still days I miss Lay Li
But it's less & less
At first my chest is on fire
The same way I feel after doing a bunch of burpees

It's like your world is shaking loose & your knees
Are shaking & you drop to the ground & think

"I'll just stay here for a while"

But no. You got to jump up

Hop on both sets of your feet

Ignore the burn

Ignore the knee ache

Reach your hands to the sky

Up

Arms reaching above your head

Up & jump

The elation you feel when you can breathe again

The burn that simmers & is just a warmth when

It's all over

    That's how I feel about Lay Li

Especially now, when I hang out with Kiyana

At first, I worry about if I'm funny enough

Then I worry about if I talk too much/not enough

It's hard being friends with people

When you are still figuring out who you are


But Kiyana is super chill

She wears her brother's hoodies

& the same pair of worn black & white Chuck Taylors

She's pretty, but doesn't seem to care about how it affects

The boys who stutter when they see her

After I play pickup with Tyrone & the others

Kiyana walks to the entrance gate & waits for me to finish

We walk back to my house so I can change before

We head to the community center

I don't go to the pool as much

Because Kiyana can't swim

We settle on going to the mall

for the second time in a week

Kiyana said "This is boring.

People just come here to look

at other people & talk smack.

Let's go to the center in Meadowview."

The center is in a part of town

that I don't normally go to.

It's hard to get there because

it's between my usual bus stops.

Kiyana shows up in her usual outfit

Faded gray hoodie, oversized & red lipstick hastily applied

It's smeared on her mouth

like she rubbed her back hand against it,

I hand her a napkin, run into the

bathroom for a quick shower


When I come out I realize Essa just walked in

Before I realize I am really hurrying to get dressed

& get out of the house before Essa can ruin my day

Or even worse, ruin my almost friendship

Out the room & up the hallway I move like a hurricane waiting

"Hey," I say. & look at Kiyana like let's get outta here.

Essa just stares at us then shrugs as Kiyana jumps up

& walks to the front door


Her eyes down down down


A block away her energy lifts in a beat

We walk past a dance studio

Where the pep squad girls for the city rehearse

All different ages of girls in sweats & bare feet

Dance at their reflection in the mirror

My beat lifts & I walk to watch them closer

Some girls snicker at us when we walk to the window

I look at Kiyana & I realize her lipstick is still smeared

My eyes are slit black beams

Ready to swing

The snickers turn to sucked teeth

Then silence.

"Kiyana, your lipstick." I point.

& just like Kiyana, she uses the sleeve of her hoodie.

"You okay?" I ask

& she inhales deep

All the oxygen must've filled her lungs

Cause she sigh in response

"Girl. Your sister is mean."

I just look at her.

Then I laugh.

I laugh so loud we have to move away from the window

I laugh until I hiccup

I laugh until my laughter got a laugh of its own

My face hurts from laughing so much

We are near the stop walk sign & I laugh

Kiyana first concerned, looks at me like I've lost my mind

Then she laughs too

& we fall into each other giggling

& we walk away towards the center

The jokes writing themselves

In the way we know the joke

Before we ever heard the punch line.

## AT THE PURNELL COMMUNITY CENTER

Our laughter sprawls like a b-boy spin

it's all spiral top

it's all sky fall

it's all gulping gulping gone, like a kitchen sink

finally free

I'm all silence

Then deep breath

& for the first time I just breathe & feel

The pat pat of my chest.

A friend is someone seeing you & hearing you

without you having to *say* everything

Every time

& in this moment

I realize I ain't never had anyone to say what my heart knows

I say "Girl, you don't even know!
My sister is the meanest person I know!"

Kiyana opens the door to the game room & a bunch of wails

spill out the opened doors. There are kids everywhere

Books everywhere

Crayons & construction paper everywhere

"She said my lipstick was ugly. Just like that."

Kiyana snaps her fingers—
"Not 'hey who are you?'
Nada.
Just something about how she didn't like my lipstick."

"I'm sorry," I start.

"No. It's okay. She seems really sad.

My brothers stay dating girls like her.

The kind of girl that needs others to be sad, so she feels better

about herself. But you're cool. You two are nothing alike."

## YOU TWO ARE NOTHING ALIKE

Nothing alike

No thing is alike

No thing is likely

I am flipping her sentence around in my head

Again & again like I'm known to do when focusing

On shooting the ball

Essa & I are nothing alike

Nothing alike

"Hey," Kiyana calls. She waves her fingers

In the air like a bouquet of ribbons.

"You okay?" she asks, her eyebrows deep creases of

concern. I smile, like it's nothing (no thing, no)

& point to the area where there is

a photo background setup.

"Let's take a photo," I say instead of "I don't know who I am.

I don't know if I'm okay. I don't know. I don't know.

But I'll figure it out."

## SELFIES BE LIKE

A couple of clicks, No

Find your angle, Oh

Find your light, No

Do not put the light behind you

It makes you darker than you really are

A couple of clicks in this position, light behind the camera

Smize, pretend no one is watching

Smirk, pretend you are a model

Smile, pretend you got all the light you need

Okay, now use flash

Now use the filter

Yes. *Vivid* that bih

Yassssss. Calm yourself with each click

Become someone more fly

Channel your inner Iman, Beyoncé, Eva, Naomi

Don't worry about who stares

you are becoming you are becoming you are you are you look like
an angel

   *look how far you've come*

## KIYANA CALLS ONE OF THEM KIDS

To come & take a photo of us both

I move my body to the front of the set

Crouch down in the front

Kiyana say "Look up."

We pose with our hands in prayer mode & we laugh

I move to the right side

Kiyana moves to the left

Green background behind us

& we pull out the peace sign

I do it to balance my bravery

"Use the flash?" the young photographer asks

We nod & both stare at the lens

Eyes unblinking

Red lips full.

Even after the bulbs flash

Dark circles swim across the room.

## AFTER WE LEAVE

The community center

Everything feels different

The air feels different

The sky feels open

I walk with Kiyana & her brother Dre

He showed up to walk us home from the bus stop

He's not so bad, I think, looking at his profile

Against the streetlight's glow

We cracking jokes & I almost forget how

quiet he be when Tyrone get to talking smack

But we can't all be heroes

I mean, even I forgot I ain't a mouse when everything

starts moving fast & arguments get loud

The only time I know I'm my own person is on the court

When I can see the game for what it is

When I know I can sit the bench & rep for my team if I can't

Keep up my pace

When I finally walk in the house, I see a note

From my mama saying dinner is on the stove

She's out with friends at the bowling alley

The phone rings & I think it's Mama checking to make sure

I made it in the house

But it's not her

It's Lay Li

& anyone eavesdropping

can hear my smile fall

When her voice crawls from the receiver.

Lay Li says "We gotta talk.

Come outside."

& before I know it

the phone is on the cradle

echoing gone through the small three-bedroom house

the screen door slams shut as I race

to my ex-bestie.

## ON THE CORNER

under a pair of streetlights

Lay Li waits under the street lamp

against the backdrop of the blue black sky.

She leans back on the steel pole

she is dipped

    wearing a fluffy pink sweatshirt

    with a Strawberry Shortcake cartoon embroidery

    where her heart would be.

Lay Li looks pale

ghost ghost pale

Her hands stuffed in the front pocket like

her nerves won't let her do much else.

"Hey," she greets me, eyes puffy

*from crying or no sleep?* I think.

It's been weeks & I realize

*I don't care. I don't care anymore.*

## BECAUSE I AIN'T DIPPED

I'm wearing last summer league's
basketball shorts & a pair of old Nike Cortez

But I ain't dipped
I don't look like Lay Li & the girls from Fashion Club
usually do, *effortless*

Nah, I look like me
& I like me

I immediately stand up straighter
like an inch can make me more memorable or more beautiful
I'd settle for just being more like me.

## LAY LI DOESN'T NOTICE MY SHORTS

Or maybe she just doesn't care

usually she'd say: "What are you wearing?"

or

"You'd look so nice in a pair of cutoff jeans"

but today          nothing

she stands under the light wringing

her hands like a dishrag.

"Hey." I nod my head

like I do when I want to play ball

or walk through the doorframe first

or get on the bus next

     or when a bunch of boys block the way.

I nod like I'm on defense.

I am defensive

I don't want to be but the way my patience is set up

The way my anxiety is set up

The way I want to fall to the ground &

Hug my stomach from all the knots

This nod will have to do.

## LAY LI OPENS HER MOUTH &
## A STORY I AIN'T NEVER WANT TO HEAR


Rushes out like a broken faucet.

She says:


Clifton tried to kiss her

& my chest fills with so much air

I think I could fill up a dozen balloons

& the knot in my gut loosens

Like when I'm on the court & the three is mines

I don't even watch it *swish*

I'm downcourt already

I already know the score.


He tried to kiss her

behind the bleachers

The same day him & I walked in the gym

I was more worried about why she ain't talk to me

I barely noticed when he left me in search of the bathroom


So how would I know

he saw her & pulled her behind the bleachers

How would I know

they knew each other from before

How would I know Lay Li

figured today, of all days, was the best

day to tell me everything.

Before things get too

out of hand.

## THE THING ABOUT THE TRUTH

is it never really surprises you

So, when Lay Li reveals what a part of me

always knew deep down in my gut

it hurts, yeah, it stings like a mugg

but what hurts more

is she waited so long.

I say: "It's been two months

& you watched me walk around

with him. It's been months

& you haven't called me back.

You saw me with him

& ain't had nothing to say?

How can you play me

when I've always had your back?

You must think I'm dumb

I was willing to fight for you just because you ask

But you were quick to let everyone make fun of me,

now you are here with this story about Clifton?

I don't care about him.

& I don't care about you.

You more concerned with what Shawn knows

& where Curtis is

than how you ain't never really been a good friend

You were like my sister

& that's why I let you walk all over me.

But I get it now, you're not my family."

Lay Li's eyes almost rolled out her head

She didn't wipe her face, just tucked her lip in

"The only reason I'm telling you is because

I know I owed you more. It wasn't right to

keep that from you. But you looked so happy.

I didn't want to hurt you that bad. Sure, it was

funny at first. To watch you sulk because I wasn't

answering your calls. But I had to deal with me

& Shawn. & that don't even matter no more.

I would never intentionally hurt you like that."

I want to stop myself from crying

I want to stop myself

But she puts a hand on my shoulder & says

"I'm truly sorry."

& the levee breaks.

## I SHOULD'VE KNOWN

Clifton was a mess

but I ain't think he was a creep.

We met at the mall

We met by the pretzel stand.

He said "Hey, Brown Sugar"

or something cheesy

& I thought he was talking to the cinnamon-covered pretzels.

We laughed.

So, when we started hanging out

I was excited someone could see my face

without Lay Li telling them to look.

Clifton looked at me

I ain't realize how important it was

until I finally felt it for myself.

But it seems Clifton looked at everybody.

It hit me

like that big ass boat & the iceberg.

I thought I could control the tears

& all the memories that come with them.

But the echoes keep me up long after

I leave Lay Li on the corner & jog back home.

I fall onto the couch, breathless

It's like I can't catch my breath.

Not even if I had a baseball mitt.

I look at the ceiling

Dancing with darkness & light beams as cars pass by

I look at the moving spots & think of how I used to move towards
the darkest corners too.

I was used to Lay Li being the center of attraction

Shoot, I helped her be in the center

My eyes on the ceiling but in my head the picture rolls:

Clifton knew Lay Li already

Lay Li already knew Clifton

In my head the picture goes:

That's why she ain't speak when we walked into the gym

That's why she ain't speak.

On the corner, I looked into Lay Li face

I mean, really looked at her

& it's the first time I've seen her cry & not

worry about how do I make it better.

I don't want to see her sad.

But I don't want to go back to my job of picking up the pieces

around her feet.

This time: her perfect makeup streaks into two rivers of black

& her perfect lipstick is

smeared into pale strips of pink

across her cheek

& on the back of her hand.

She reaches to move her bangs out her face

& a footprint of pink is left on her forehead too.

## HER EYES THEN FIXED

on the cold black ground
unmoving under our feet.

Still the air is hot
like a balloon ride to nowhere

& Lay Li can't look at me.
Cousin Inga says never trust a person

that can't look me in the eyes
& I want to believe it's that easy.

But what if someone can't look at you
because they heart is broken too?

Or what if someone can't look at you
because they can't face the truth?

Or what if someone can't look at you
because it's hard to stand up for the right thing?

Everybody wants to be a hero, but most of us
are just misunderstood villains.

It's like Lay Li can hear me arguing with my blood.

She lifts her eyes

Sad & brown.

This time she doesn't look away.

She just exhales loud & slow

Like she's waiting for the other shoe to drop

& that's when I know the difference between the truth

& a lie.

## LIKE THE TIME

Ronique told that lie
about not liking Russ

like the time
Serenity told that lie about not liking Ronique

like the time
Inga said she ain't watch them hit that girl at the bus stop

like the time
I walked a different way so I could talk to Justin

like the time
I walked a different way so I could talk to Irving

like the time
Raymond said he didn't know I was afraid of snakes

like the time
Lay Li's father came home early
& she said she was alone asleep

like the time
Mama said Daddy would be home soon

like the time
the politicians said they would fix the softball field

like the time
the superintendent said they would remove the metal detectors

like the time
the nurse said it's okay it's okay it's okay    —just breathe

like the time
we had to learn how to hide our bodies
between bookcases in the dark
during the school intruder drill

like the time
Uncle Lenny punched Russ square in the chest

like the time
Russ said it didn't hurt

like the time
Russ said he ain't even cry

like the time
we told Mama nothing happened

like the time
I said I didn't find the ashtray under Essa's bed

like the time
I said I wasn't drinking beer

like the time
I said I wasn't smoking

like the time
I said I wasn't exactly who I am.

## LAY LI'S HANDS SPEAK A LANGUAGE TOO

with both palms moving as she tells me the story

right hand & left hand

swinging on each side of her body.

they are comma

comma

exclamation point

comma

exclamation

dash

ellipses . . .

    He tried to kiss me

    He tried to kiss me

    He tried to kiss me

I know you like him

      I didn't want it

        I didn't want it

          I didn't

He tried to kiss me

He said he heard about me

He tried to kiss me

    He pushed me in the corner

beneath the bleachers

I couldn't move

    He tried to kiss me

    His hands were so big

    His eyes were so dark

    He said no one would believe me.

& so

    He kissed me

    All hot & pushy

    His tongue was too wet

    I didn't want it

    I didn't want him

    His hands grabbed my sweatshirt

    Gripped it like a bat

Gripped it like I betta not

move

He wouldn't stop
I couldn't make him

     stop
I'm so sorry

Don't cry
Don't cry
Don't cry

## IT'S FINALLY SATURDAY

& I barely make it through the week

The heat wave has crawled up the Valley hills

& put its feet up

That means it's going to be here awhile

In California, the weather will match your temper

if you ain't careful

Today

It's too hot to think

& I ain't got time to teach the boys to mind they hands

Who else gets to walk around with their putting they hands

on things that don't belong to them?

## I JUST WANT TO HOOP

I want to do something that ain't got nothing to do with
being a girl.

I want to do something that don't give folks a right to tell me
To sit quiet
Or be still
Or play small
I don't want to play small.

I think of Lay Li
How mighty her mouth is
How she walks in & the room go silent
How she is like a boss.

But now I realize she ain't the boss.
Now I realize it's all a trick
Now I realize being a girl is heavy business.

It's like a basketball game with no referee
Just two teams & everybody play by they own rules

People only care about winning

You have to mind the ball or the gravity

But people only care about winning

They don't care who they take from

They don't care about how foul they be

So you pivot & protect

yourself

Until something or someone else comes for you

& they foul & double dribble & challenge you like a bully

But when you do it back—they call you a bad sport.

## AIN'T NO MORE PLAYING SMALL

Ain't no more being still

Ain't no more being quiet

Ain't no more time for all of that

I want to do something that don't tell folks

They have a right to tell me who I am.

I won't be treated differently because I'm a girl

& today everything changes.

## TYRONE SEES ME FIRST

His anger wants to be hotter than the sun
But his balls & his stomach know better.

Kiyana is by the blacktop talking to Dre
when I walk up
She can tell something is up
"Meet up later?" she asks, walking away
"Cool," I say.

Tyrone sneers
"You betta not come talking mess."

I sneer back
"We playing ball or what?"

## TODAY ON THE COURT

I put all my energy into dribbling clean
I put all my energy into passing the ball

Dre & I against the world.
Today

The world is Tyrone & some lowerclassmen with height
Who smell bad.

I try not to think about what Lay Li told me
I try not to think how I went looking for Clifton
Ready to fight.
I try to focus on dribbling clean
I try to focus on anything but the dull pain in my chest
I try to focus on my feet not being stuck to the concrete.
I raise my hands with the ball lifted off the ground
peep Dre's position & pass him the rock.

## ABOUT FRIDAY NIGHT

I found Clifton at the mall on Friday, right?
& he laughing with his friends, not a care in the world
He pretend he ain't see me & Lay Li.
He act like everything is sugar sweet dumpling molasses
"Hey, babe." He slithered towards me

Before he recognized Lay Li tearstained face was walking
with me

Before he could see Lay Li face was set in stone
Clifton looked past her & right at me
"I don't know what she said but . . ."
I didn't even let him finish.

I grabbed his large cup of soda & spilled it everywhere.
Some of the fruit-punch red landed on his beloved kicks.

Lay Li grabbed the pretzels & tossed them in the air
Like flower petals or rice at a wedding.

The expensive pretzel bites & cheese salted bread

fell in a gooey mess on his red & white sweatshirt

& lie in front of his feet.

His frown took over his whole face

His friends laughed & clapped hands behind him

"Brooooooooo" is all we heard as we walked toward the exit.

The security guard didn't even look at us twice.

We headed out the door into the night's darkening blue.


"Thank you for believing me,"

Lay Li said.


I couldn't say a word

My throat was too constricted with all the tears

& words I wanted to say


I couldn't do anything but nod

as we climbed the stairs of bus 62 in silence

grabbing a seat on opposite sides for our last

bus ride home.

## AFTER A PICKUP GAME

The walk used to feel like a desert stretched far away
from home.

It's how I always ended up at Lay Li's house.

Ten blocks home & I could walk into my own house
& argue with Essa.
But who wants to do that every week?
Not me.

Just a couple of blocks to Lay Li's I could find a seat
& some peace from all the noise.

Today, I walk home even though I'm tired
Even though Lay Li & I have squashed our differences.
I just need time to think to myself
Kiyana is waiting for me in front of the pool
Usually, I'm down to jump in & let the water wash
everything again
Today, I'm crowded with all my own thinking

I don't want to swim

I don't want to talk

I just want to sleep it off.

Kiyana shakes her head. "You don't look so good. What happened?

Maybe you should go home & rest."

I just need time to think

Without the voice-mail light blinking from Clifton's ignored calls.

I just need time to myself

& I don't want to think on the doubts that wait patiently for me

Like outfits that stare back from my closet laughing

at who I think I am.

I just need time to think

but not about Tyrone

who said I thought I was better than boys

& needed to be put in my place

I just need time to think

but I don't want to think about

Tyrone who promised

to put me in my place

with the help of his cousin,

Clifton

Tyrone & Clifton think they can shame me

& make me feel small.

I just need time to think

but not about Lay Li & Shawn & Curtis

or how after she saw me mistreated

she look more & more like my sister,

Essa, or how after all that I still wanted

to protect her. Because I know what it's

like to be alone. Really alone.

I look at Kiyana, who hasn't moved

or said a word. She just listens, her

eyes watering—I must look crazy.

She can't be crying for me . . .

"I feel like I can't breathe," I say & choke back tears,

but it sounds like *I feel like I can't be.*

## THE NEXT MORNING


I woke with my eyes swollen

& still red.

My room had pictures of my heroes on the wall

Opposite my bed

Method Man & Missy Elliott

Serena Williams & LeBron James

Lisa Leslie & Steph Curry

Misty Copeland & Drake

Side by side they sat

My guardian angels.


I keep Fannie Lou Hamer

& Oprah & Cardi B on my door

So when I walk out

I would carry the swag of Cardi

the fight of Fannie Lou

& the boss attitude of Oprah.

But this morning

Even my angels can't get me hype

Basketball shorts in hand

& my old summer camp tee slung over

My sports bra.

I run to the bathroom

Brush my teeth

& move to the front door

Essa is in the kitchen

She say "You want some?"

& points to the pan of scrambled eggs with cheese.

This is not normal

But last night something clicked in us both.

As soon as I walked in the door

She started her usual tactics

Talking smack

Talking fast

"Why you look like that?!

You need to act like

You got a home walking in all
Like a disaster."

Usually this starts the war
But my head hurts & my feelings hurt
& now that I know what I need to know
about Clifton
I don't even blink at the sarcasm falling
from her mouth
Essa stop talking & look at me.
I mean really stares at me for the first time.
Her face twitches & then it's like all the
meanness in her face just drains
down dirt down to the floor.

## ALL THE THINGS PEOPLE SAY TO ME & ABOUT ME

has beat me down.

"I'm tired"

I sigh

"I'm tired"

I say

"Essa, you got an issue with me

& I have tried everything

You my sister

But you not my friend

It's clear

You rather talk bad to me

Than teach me how to take care of myself

I'm so small around you

& you still hate me

I would blame you for everything

the way I let people walk over me

I would blame you for everything

but that would change nothing

It's clear

You hate me

You so hateful

& I don't know why

I've tried everything

I would fight the world for you

But I can't keep fighting you

My arms too tired."

Essa's eyebrows are lifted

sky sky up & then she sighs too.

"I'm just playing, dang. It's not that serious."

That was last night.

& that was that.

This morning, though,

I simply snatch an apple from the fruit bowl

& almost smile & shake my head.

"I'm good"

I lie

& fly out the door.

## DAMN!

my knees wobble from the hour-long game

my back

& hands

& elbows

ache like an exposed nerve

my tooth feels loose.

I care less about the tooth

& more about the losing.

I tried my best

but Tyrone's big brother came to play ball too.

They boxed me out

two big-ass refrigerator-sized walls

it's like they both from a family of cast-iron skillets

& skyscrapers

& rottweilers

but I don't know how to back down from a fight

even when I know I will never win.

Afterwards, Dre helped me up & I called game

I know when it's over

I know when the show is done.

I walked off the court, limping & head high

I wiped my face with the T-shirt corner & moved slowly

towards my long walk back home.

I'd skip the pool today

Lonely feels like that

Until

I hear Dre calling Tyrone weak-minded

I look back & see them square up

Tyrone's brother is in the middle of them both

a brick wall of a freshman in community college

just trying to keep the peace.

## INGA SAYS

Play smarter.

You can't beat everyone

Sure

You may outrun someone

    but they always catch up.

You can outthink

    but they always catch on.

If they box you out

    You make a new box

    You make them play your game.

Think of your team

What are their strengths?

What are your strengths?

Now play smart    not small

Think quick but think good

You have everything you need

Where's the rock?

Focus.

Breathe.

Sprint.

Focus.

Leap.

Focus.

Dribble.

Where are you?

In your head?

No

You got to be two steps ahead of the strongest adversary

Be two steps ahead of anyone that tries to put you down because
you're a girl

    Being a Black girl & a Black girl baller is a whole set of rules

    you never see coming

    Know the rules

    So you know which ones you need to break

Are you a baller?

Then honor the baller.

Play your position.

Let your team be a team.

Let them be their best selves.

Your endurance is not your only ability

Your strength is not to run fast or ball the hardest

Your superpower is to see what your team needs

& show up for them.

Be agile

Cause you can!

You got to keep swinging, Lil' Cousin

because you're the real prize.

& those that respect you & love you

will keep it one hundred

won't play you small or play you at all.

Remember, somebody see you, even

when the sky looks pitch black & you can't

see the outline of your own hand

even when there are so many moving

parts & you can't find the man on your team

You're never really alone.

See, a real leader knows

there is no such thing as a one-person team!

If you think there is

you've already lost

Everything is a game

Some folks be playing to win the house, the job,
the car, the spotlight

Everything is a game to be won but some of us
are playing for things that last longer than material things

Once you figure out what you gaming for

Then you can play honest & with integrity

If you show up & show the world your real self

You don't have to wait for others to claim you

You don't have to wait for others to pick you

You pick yourself, I mean

Really choose yourself every day

& no one will be able to tell you

that you aren't the real MVP.

## SKY SAYS

It's like all my life

I've let how others feel about me

Tell me how I feel about myself

ONLY today it feels different

    The air feels more clean

    The sun feels more heat skillet stove top

Today is different

    I can hear Inga in my head telling me how to hold my hands
    & how to play defense

    I can still see my mama's smile when I tell her we won the game

    I can still see Essa shake her head at me when I walk in

    I can still see Lay Li look then not look in my direction

Before Today

    I take too long to think about what it all means

    I take so much time thinking about if somebody is mad at me

    I take my time back

    I am not forgettable

    I get to be here

Right here & now

    I get to take up space too

    I get to plant my feet firmly on this skillet pan of a blacktop

Take a deep breath

Extend my arms

    Like a statue

    Like a ballerina

    Like good money

    Like an octave up the bleachers

*SWISH*

    Like a girl at the homecoming dance

    Like a girl dancing with her own self in the mirror

    Like that's my song

    Like that's my smile

    Like that's my heart

    Like I like me

    Like I can look in the mirror &

    Like my own me

    Like me

    Like me

    Like me

Today is different

    Because I say it is mine

    The sky is mine

    My name is mine

    I am Sky &

    I got now

# Acknowledgments

I exist because of Cora Maxine Craig, Elsie Jean Tims, and Ellaine Toni Jackson. I survived because these women illuminated the path. To my cousin Tiffany Walter, you are not only a cousin but a sister; not only a sister but a blueprint to the kind of woman I would become. I love you.

My writing begins each day with gratitude for family and friends. For Beyoncé sing-offs and DJ diatribes. J, you are the only way. Amari, you are the only way. Thank you for championing me and my smallest achievements. I love you. I know love because of your love.

To all the folks who gave me space to write: Bearing Witness Fellowship at Art for Justice Fund; AIR Serenbe; Cave Canem; Poets House; O, Miami; Rauschenberg Residency; Urban Word NYC; and Young Chicago Authors.

I am forever honored to have witnessed the world that Jacqueline Woodson made possible for my Black Girl Bloom. I am super thankful for Nic Stone and her hand in my journey to Crown Books. Thank you, Phoebe Yeh, for seeing my light and making sure there was room for me in this lit world. Thank you, Crown family, for supporting my every marketing and cover art desire.

Thank you to my forever beacons: my agent, Charlotte Sheedy, and the watchful eye of Ally Sheedy. Who would I become in this lit world without your excellence? I love you both dearly. Thank you.

My friends—Oakland to Sacramento to Pasadena to Hollywood to Philly to Baltimore to Miami to Atlanta to Dominica to Flatbush to the BX to Bangladesh to Brooklyn. I love you. I am you.

I am ever grateful for my first line of literary defense, my editing guru, and my brother in pen, Jason Reynolds. *This* book could not exist without you. My place in the YA world would not exist without your insistence that my voice and story is needed. Thank you for the Brownstone sermons. I owe you.

# About the Author

**MAHOGANY L. BROWNE** is a poet, an organizer, the author of several children's books, and the founder of the Woke Baby Book Fair. Her first novel in verse, *Chlorine Sky,* is inspired by the beauty of the California landscape that raised her and the basketball courts that taught her to stand up for herself. If she isn't returning to high school photos to forgive her younger self, she is roaming the streets of Brooklyn, New York, listening to Kendrick Lamar and Leikeli47. She feels most balanced watching *The Amazing World of Gumball.*

mobrowne.com